To Jan ! ♡

♡ Nancy Carl

1990

WATCH OUT
FOR THESE
WEIRDOS!

Rufus Kline
Pictures by Nancy Carlson

Viking

VIKING
Published by the Penguin Group
Viking Penguin, a division of Penguin Books USA Inc.,
40 West 23rd Street, New York, New York 10010, U.S.A.
Penguin Books Ltd, 27 Wrights Lane, London W8 5TZ, England
Penguin Books Australia Ltd, Ringwood, Victoria, Australia
Penguin Books Canada Ltd, 2801 John Street, Markham, Ontario, Canada L3R 1B4
Penguin Books (N.Z.) Ltd, 182–190 Wairau Road, Auckland 10, New Zealand

Penguin Books Ltd, Registered Offices: Harmondsworth, Middlesex, England

First published in 1990 by Viking Penguin, a division of Penguin Books USA Inc.

10 9 8 7 6 5 4 3 2 1

Text copyright © Rufus Kline, 1990
Illustrations copyright © Nancy Carlson, 1990
All rights reserved

Library of Congress Cataloging in Publication Data
Kline, Rufus.   Watch out for these weirdos
Rufus Kline ; pictures by Nancy Carlson. p.   cm.
Summary: Wanted posters introduce a gallery of offbeat characters,
including Erin "Starin" McCarron who looks in people's windows and
Bob "The Slob" McCobb who was once buried under the mess in his room.
ISBN 0-670-82376-7 [1. Humorous stories.] I. Carlson, Nancy L., ill. II. Title.
PZ7.K6794Wat   1990 [E]—dc20   89-37865

Printed in Japan.
Set in Zapf Book Light.

In case you move into my neighborhood, watch out for these weirdos.

WANTED

ERIN *"STARIN"* McCARRON

AGE: 7

HEIGHT: Mostly short, but taller when she stands on a stool or something.

WEIGHT: She watches it carefully.

HAIR: She keeps it out of her eyes.

EYES: Always on something.

FAVORITE SAYING: "Can I see that?"

WANTED FOR: Making you nervous when she stares at you.

LATEST CRIME: Looking in the neighbor's front window all night long.

APPROACH WITH CAUTION: If you don't watch your step, she will.

This is Erin who's always staring.

WANTED

RYAN "*CRYIN*" O'BRIEN

AGE: 5

HEIGHT: Too short.

WEIGHT: Too small.

HAIR: Curly.

EYES: Full of tears.

FAVORITE SAYING: "Waaaaaaah!"

WANTED FOR: Keeping the whole neighborhood up all night.

LATEST CRIME: Making his parents leave a restaurant before they were finished eating.

APPROACH WITH CAUTION: Best to wear earmuffs.

This is Ryan who's always crying.

WANTED

SUSAN "*MONKEY GIRL*" LA GAMBA

AGE: 9

HEIGHT: Tall enough to reach tree branches.

WEIGHT: Light enough to swing easily.

HAIR: Full of leaves.

EYES: 2

FAVORITE SAYING: "Bet you can't do this."

WANTED FOR: Swinging on things and knocking stuff over.

LATEST CRIME: Doing an ape call when the teacher was out of the room.

APPROACH WITH CAUTION: She might jump up and swing on you.

This is Sue who belongs in the zoo.

WANTED

WILLIAM *"SILLY WILLY"* BARILLI

AGE: 6

HEIGHT: About right.

WEIGHT: Too skinny. He's always giggling so much he can't eat.

HAIR: Gum in it.

EYES: Crossed a lot.

FAVORITE SAYING: "I know you are but what am I?"

WANTED FOR: Not sitting quietly and paying attention.

LATEST CRIME: Putting sand in Sandra's lunch box.

APPROACH WITH CAUTION: He drops stuff down your back.

This is Willy who always acts silly.

WANTED

"*TATTLIN*" MADELINE BROWN

AGE: 8

HEIGHT AND WEIGHT: She doesn't know her own, but she knows everybody else's.

HAIR: Never brushes it. She's too busy telling on people.

EYES: Always looking for ways to get you in trouble.

FAVORITE SAYING: "I'm gonna tell."

WANTED FOR: Getting checks after people's names.

LATEST CRIME: Telling on Bob for leaving his lunch tray on the table.

DON'T BOTHER TO APPROACH WITH CAUTION: No matter what you do, she's going to tell on you.

This is Madeline who's always tattling.

WANTED
RICHARD "SICKY RICKY" VALICKI

AGE: 9

HEIGHT: Not sure. He doesn't feel well enough to stand up straight.

WEIGHT: Skinny because he says he has a stomachache and can't eat.

HAIR: Usually messy because he's too tired to comb it.

EYES: Always looking for a place to lie down.

FAVORITE SAYING: "Hey, school's out! I feel a lot better!"

WANTED FOR: Never finishing his schoolwork.

LATEST CRIME: Getting out of a spelling test, because his head hurt.

APPROACH WITH CAUTION: Don't ask him how he is—you don't want
    to hear it.

This is Rick who says he's always sick.

WANTED

GARY *"THE VAMPIRE"* JONES

AGE: 8

HEIGHT: Tall enough to cast a shadow in the moonlight.

WEIGHT: Not heavy enough. He says he doesn't get enough blood.

HAIR: Slicked down to look like Dracula.

EYES: Always looking for his next victim.

FAVORITE SAYING: "It's midnight! The monster awakes!"

WANTED FOR: Always trying to scare the little kids in kindergarten.

LATEST CRIME: Telling everybody that his tomato juice was really blood.

APPROACH WITH CAUTION: He doesn't like it if you laugh when he tries
    to scare you.

This is Gary who tries to act scary.

WANTED

JENNIFER *"GET YOUR OWN MONEY"* BANKS

AGE: 8

WEIGHT: Pretty heavy when you count her purse full of coins.

HAIR: Long. Saves money on haircuts.

EYES: Good at watching her pennies.

FAVORITE SAYING: "How much does that cost?"

WANTED FOR: Never sharing anything.

LATEST CRIME: Eating ice cream in front of her friends.

WARNING! Don't approach at all if you want to borrow something.

This is Jenny who won't lend you a penny.

WANTED

ROBERT *"BOB THE SLOB"* McCOBB

AGE: 10

HEIGHT: Tall enough to see over the pile of junk in his room.

WEIGHT: Way too heavy if you count all the junk he stuffs in his pocket.

HAIR: Ice cream, gravy, and mustard in it.

EYES: Never sees anything to clean up.

FAVORITE SAYING: "Okay! Okay! I'll pick it up."

WANTED FOR: Being the world's biggest slob.

LATEST CRIME: Having a desk full of candy wrappers, apple cores, and old orange peels.

APPROACH WITH CAUTION: If he's eating, he'll probably get food on you.

This is Bob who acts like a slob.

WANTED

ANTHONY *"TONY BALONEY"* WELLS

AGE: 9

HEIGHT: A foot shorter than he says it is.

HAIR: Always combed the way he says the bigshots do it.

EYES: Always seeing things that aren't there.

FAVORITE SAYING: "Ah, that's nothing. Wait till you hear this."

WANTED FOR: For saying he was going to drive everybody around the block in his Dad's car.

LATEST CRIME: Saying he couldn't eat his brussels sprouts because secret guys from outer space put stuff in them.

APPROACH WITH CAUTION: Believe him at your own risk.

This is Tony who's full of baloney.

WANTED
EDWARD *"ALWAYS LATE"* BATES

AGE: 10

HEIGHT: Too short to get a good look at the clock.

WEIGHT: He was not on time when they weighed everybody, so we
don't know.

HAIR: Growing slowly.

EYES: Not quite open.

FAVORITE SAYING: "Huh?"

WANTED FOR: Never being on time.

LATEST CRIME: No one knows. He didn't show up for it.

APPROACH WITH CAUTION: You may wake him up.

This is Eddie who's never ready.

But don't say anything bad about them. . . .

Because they're my friends.